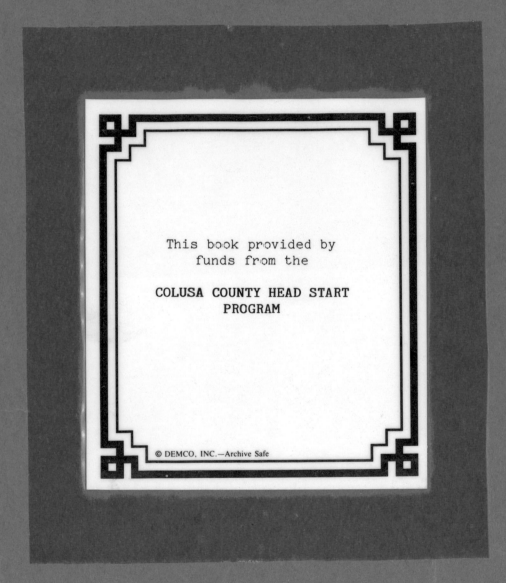

When Crocodiles Clean Up

by Roni Schotter
illustrated by Thor Wickstrom

Macmillan Publishing Company   New York
Maxwell Macmillan Canada   Toronto
Maxwell Macmillan International
New York   Oxford   Singapore   Sydney

Library of Congress Cataloging-in-Publication Data
Schotter, Roni. When crocodiles clean up / by Roni Schotter ; illustrated by Thor Wickstrom. — 1st ed.   p.   cm.
Summary: When their mother orders them to clean up their room, rambunctious young crocodiles do so with some
unorthodox methods. ISBN 0-02-781297-9 [1. Crocodiles —Fiction. 2. Orderliness—Fiction.] I. Wickstrom, Thor,
ill. II. Title. PZ7.S3765Wh 1993   [E]—dc20   92-10808

For Diana Engel;
artist, writer, and, best of all, friend
—R.S.

To my sister Valerie,
and all her little crocodiles
—T.W.

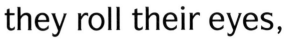

they roll their eyes,

thwack their tails,

and bellow…

When no one's around,
they crunch crackers,
jaw jellies,
and tear into toast.

They slither and slide,

and play hide-and-creep.

They grin

and grunt

and grab,

fret and fight,

and then make up.

They sing marsh melodies

and lie belly-up in bed dreaming of summer

and the swamp.

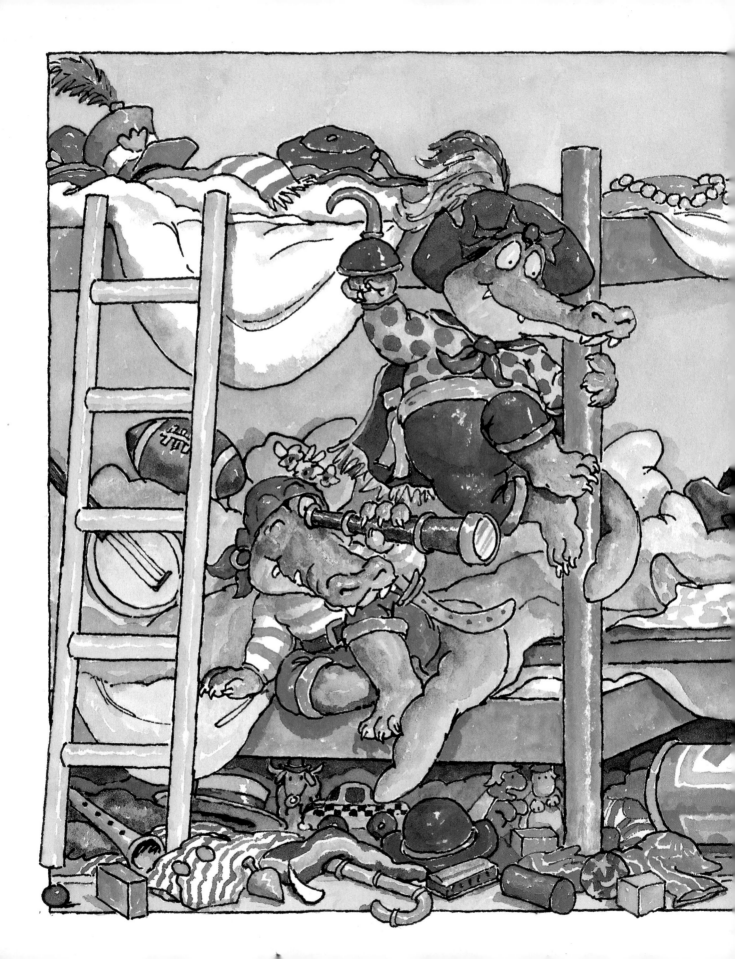

They play pirate.

When crocodiles clean up . . .